CITIZEN DWEEB
Dog Poop for the Sole

CITIZEN DWEEB
Dog Poop for the Sole

STAN NELSON

Psycho_Babble Productions / Seattle

ISBN:

Edited and Layout by Brian Michael Hall
Front and Back Covers by Bob Shook
Photo by Amanda Nelson

First Edition

For Parker and Amanda

CONTENTS

Forward

Just a quick yarn from the VHF marine radio. Name's Ezekiel Bonesteel, been masterin' the decks and trimmin' the sails on the Nefarious, cruisin' the Salish Sea for a solid thirty-eight years.

Let's have a chinwag about Stan Nelson. This bloke, he ain't no suck-up. He'd sooner hit the deck and have a go at a filthy pair of runners with his gob than grovel. Reckon he'd use that tongue of his, sharp and split like a serpent's, to do the trick!

But don't get it twisted, he ain't no sycophant. Nah, mate. Stan's the type to wing it, cruisin' through life in his stubbies. When he popped the question about spinnin' my tales, I told him, "Yeah, mate, but first show me some of that sneaker action."

And don't forget to tip your hat to Antonio J. Hopson. That legend was the first to scribble down my sea farin' tales, makin' my name known like them Bible blokes did for old mate Lazarus, or what Steinbeck did with Ed Ricketts and his sea critters.

Treat Stan's scribblin' with the same gravitas as a Honey Badger faces off with a bit of venom—tough as nails, that one. If it don't knock him dead, he's back at it, scoffin' down brekkie like a champ. Good on ya, Stan! Chuck that art down ya, cop a beauty of a stupor, and if it don't finish ya, whizz it out and get crackin' on the next yarn.

Catch ya later for a few cold ones.

Cheers and hooroo,

Ezekiel Bonesteel

"Words in prose ought to express the intended meaning; if they attract attention to themselves, it is a fault. In the very best styles you read page after page without noticing the medium. Works of imagination should be written in very plain language; the more purely imaginative they are, the more necessary it is to be plain."

-Samuel Taylor Coleridge

"I feel sorry for people who are easily offended and too sensitive to laugh at poop jokes."

-John Stefnik

1

It Rhymes with Lurkey

- I'm going to start doing some book signings. You bring some books of your choice and I'll sign them.

- Let's get this straight, folks. Salt and pepper shakers are only salt and pepper holders. People are the salt and pepper shakers.

- The Ouija Board is a device that is believed by some people to communicate with the dead by spelling out words and messages on the board.
I have a Squeegee Board that can spell out words and messages onto my windshield when it rains.

- "Money talks, bullshit walks." Now I can handle the talking money part but if I see poop walking around, I'm heading for the hills.

- A popular rule of thumb while driving is to keep your hands at the 10 o'clock and 2 o'clock positions on the steering wheel. Is that p.m. to a.m. or a.m. to p.m.? I need to know; that's a difference of half of a day. I can't be driving around twelve hours late for everything.

- A large sum of money makes a whole lot of cents.

- I like to call restaurants that specialize in Native American food and ask them if I need a reservation to eat there.

- Some experts say that dogs have the ability to smell cancer in humans. Although it's nothing that we can ever rely on for detection purposes yet, but if there's any truth to this, I'll tell you right now, based on hundreds of previous K9 grundle sniffings, I must have some serious crotch cancer.

- Why do some old people have a box of tissue by the back window of their car? I specifically said "old" so you can picture what kind of car it is. That ever so distant box of tissue will do you no good if you sneeze and a chunk of DNA lands on your wrist while you are driving to the pharmacy to pick up some salve for your anal warts. Or, while driving to work, your body decides to have a coughing fit and you hook a piece of breakfast sausage onto the inside of the windshield. Again, that box of tissue way back by the rear window is not going to help you one bit.

- Here's an odd feeling, try reading a children's book while drinking a can of beer. It's freaky. It's like watching ass porn and talking to your mom on the phone at the same time. It defies logic and should never be done.

- A "hop, skip, and a jump" seems innocent and cute, until you're standing three feet from a moving train.

- Cheech and Chong are a perfect example of being double jointed.

- **AAAAAAAA**
The Octuple A Club.
Battery operated, alcohol free, roadside assistance.

- With the power of words, I am now going to put an image in your head that I guarantee you have never thought of before. Are you ready? Now picture this............a cow shitting like a dog.

- You can guess the confusion this caused when aging rock star Huey Lewis became a news anchor at **KROK** News.
"......and at 6 o'clock, Huey Lewis and the news."
"Hey Marge! Get your ass in here right now! Huey Lewis and the News are going to rock our socks off in a few minutes."

- Have you ever heard the stupid line "All that and a bag of chips"? As in *she's* all that and a bag of chips. I honestly don't think that sounds very spectacular, I mean really, it's just a bag of potato chips folks, that's not saying much at all. Now if you were in a casino with a bag of chips, that's a bag of chips worth adding extra emphasis to.

- I believe all the pot stores here in the state of Washington could have greatly benefited in getting this word "instagram" trademarked, especially if they had a drive through.
"Welcome to Bud's Bud Hut can I take your order?"
"Yeah, I'll take the instagram, and make it snappy because I have to throw a whiz."
"That will be a shit load of money at the second window."

- I'm cooking a pork butt and the recipe calls for a dry meat rub. I'll give it my best, but I don't see what that has to do with cooking.

- "Thank you for having your radio dial tuned in to 98.5 KSUN the home of blue skies and all smiles, feel good hits on feel good radio! This is Kansas with Dust In The Wind…"

- For shits and giggles, I tried to learn how to tie a noose, but I quickly gave it up. I didn't want to get all hung up on it.

- I want to crunch some numbers, doesn't that sound cool? You hear that line in movies, usually pertaining to somebody in a suit trying to sell something for a butt-load of money. Anyways, I really am in the mood to "crunch some numbers," but I have no numbers to crunch. So, I bought a box of Alpha-Bits cereal and will have to settle for crunching some letters.

- I have noticed that when I see a group of bicyclists or joggers, the person in the back always looks miserable and has a purplish hue to their face.

- Venereola:
It's a hybrid of venereal and areola.
That's all, I just made that shit up, you
didn't, so there!

- I question any sauce that comes in a
clear jar and looks like a thick reddish
pile of embryonic glop and is called
Prego.

- I put a urinal in my back yard which
really pisses my neighbors off because I
like to use it from my second story
balcony.

- To the wiminz,
I find it very appropriate for you to yell
"FOOTBALLS!" during the exact
moment you are kicking some loser right
in his nuts.

- What the hell did this Jehovah guy do?
And why does he need so many
witnesses?

2

They Have Totally Different Things in Common

- I was just thinking, I have never done the Crocodile Rock. Am I missing out on something cool?
I've done the Locomotion, I've done the Time Warp, I've done the Hokey Pokey, the Jitterbug, the Mashed Potato, the Toxic Waltz, the Walk of Life, the Twist, the Puyallup, the Freak Nasty, and I even She Bopped and Danced with Myself.
But I have yet to do the thing called the Crocodile Rock.

- The Beatles ruined Yoko Ono.

- Great news! I now have Wi-Fi in my pants!

- In Kentucky, it is illegal to carry ice cream in your back pocket, yep, that shit is real folks.

- After doing a little research on fracking, I have to say that I am opposed to that frickin' fracking.

- Here's a great test to find out if someone is an alcoholic, its easy.
Get said person buzzed and take their alcohol away from them. Now hand them a tall glass of some warm foamy yellowish liquid.
Is it beer? Or is it piss? Either way if they start guzzling it then they are an alcoholic.
Enjoy that piss!

- My stomach just made a noise so loud that it can only mean one thing. There is an emergency in my very near future and I'm glad I am at home right now.

- It's difficult to explain my sense of humor to kleptomaniacs because they might take it literally.

- Betty Shatrod was the first recipient to receive a prosthetic neck. It was deemed a total success for about, oh............nine seconds.

- While serving in the *army*, Russell *Arm*strong lost one *arm* trying to dis*arm* the enemy of their *arms*. Perhaps if he was wearing *arm*or, Russell *Arm*strong wouldn't have lost his *arm* while trying to dis*arm* the enemy of their *arm*s while serving in the *army*.

- Speaking of binary code, if you want to add a butt-load of zeros and ones to your savings account, just deposit your monies into a data bank.

Hey! That was clever shit right there, just because you didn't laugh at it doesn't mean it wasn't clever.

- I would like to start off by saying I do not want any fanfare, gifts, or cards with cash in them. But I am very happy to announce that after many years of hard work I have now received my master's degree in reverse psychology.

Please remember, I want absolutely no cards with cash in them. Thank you.

- The older I get, the more my farts sound like Jello suction.

- There's an air stagnation advisory in my pants.

- If you study a star map of the night sky, you may find Labia Majora and Labia Minora. What the hell? Are those girl parts or star constellations?

- Doesn't a Graham Cracker sound like a Caucasian pot dealer? No? OK.

- I don't see why it's a big deal to change my socks, I don't think it does any good switching them from right to left and left to right.

- No Joshua! I would not like to play chess; I want to play Global Thermonuclear War.

- It took me a couple of times to figure this out, that anytime one of my dumb dogs quickly turns around and looks at its own asshole, it's time to open up every window in the house.
#deathbydogfarts

- In my world, "Ctrl + Alt + Delete" = the big cyber-finger.

- Here's a question that is directed towards those who pee standing up. Why is there always a big ol' nasty booger smeared on the wall directly above the urinal?

- I have always thought that "slut," "whore," "gutter tramp," and all the other names of that sort were quite awful sounding. How about a more pleasant name like "the dick whisperer?"

- And in today's news, actor, director, and writer James "Doo-Doo" Johnson was found dead yesterday in his Los Angeles apartment where he obtained seventeen single gunshot wounds, numerous stab wounds, two shotgun blasts to the groin, and a shoe was found lodged in his esophagus.

Although it appears to be an accident, authorities are not ruling out homicide.

James appeared in twenty-nine films and several commercials, but was best known for writing, directing, and staring in his instructional video series "Pooping Is Fun."

James was 46 years old.

- Jimmy Buffett mini-series 1 of 3
"It's Nobody's Fault"

- Jimmy Buffett mini-series 2 of 3
"It Could Be My Fault"

- Jimmy Buffett mini-series 3 of 3
"It's My Own Damn Fault"

- There's a sandwich board sign on the side of the road that reads "flat tire $7." That's where folks pull inside and a gentleman comes running up to the car, collects the seven dollars and proceeds to put a knife through their tire, then runs back.

- Coming this summer to a theater near you! A movie so scary you will literally shit yourself.

- My promise to you - yeah *you* - you're reading this right now, aren't you? I promise that I will not use the words isotope, zeitgeist, algorithm, and entropy in this book.
Well, starting NOW, I won't use those words.

- Are Secular communities and Atheist churches considered non prophet organizations?

- While driving home from buying some extra-strength, antifungal rash cream today, I heard an interview on the radio with a guy that was very upset about a removal project of sorts. He was so pissed off that he never even explained what was being removed, he just kept referring to that dam removal project.

- For health reasons alone, obese people don't necessarily make good role models, but they do make great roll models. See where I went with that?

- Products that might not sell well #9
    - Night vision gloves
    - Nose pens
    - Love retardant cologne
    - Glass ladder
    - Battery operated kite
    - Popcorn slicer
    - Stool retractor gun
    - Pressure washer with water pick, toothbrush, and enema-attachments.

- One of many great things about K-9 police dogs is when they catch some criminal asshole and pull him to the ground by violently tugging on his nuts.

- I have actually played Kick the Can. And you know what? It was really fun. That's all.

- I'm getting really tired of doing what Simon says. Simon says this, Simon says that. For years now I've been doing what Simon says, sit down, stand up, rub my belly, stand on one leg. Who the hell does he think he is anyway? I've had it with that bossy no good turd. It's time we silence Simon once and for all.
Stan says, "Shut the hell up Simon."

- I believe Professor Plum did it in the bathroom with his pipe.

- Where did the word "supper" go? How come nobody uses that anymore?

3

Martha is Cold

- Heading into California across the Nevada border, I approached the agriculture inspection station where they check your vehicle to see if you are carrying any fruits or vegetables over the state line. I immediately broke out in a nervous cold sweat because about twenty miles back I had picked up Richie Simmons and Steven Hawking while they were hitchhiking.
Names have been altered to protect my ass from being spanked by the gods of publishing.

- No! Your honor, I did not punch Mr. Farnsworth, I simply spanked his face with my fist.

- Here's the real six degrees of Kevin Bacon.
1. Associate of Arts
2. Bachelor of Fine Arts
3. Doctoral of Finer Arts
4. PhD of the Finest Arts
5. Masters of Advanced Most Finest Arts
6. ASS of Political Science

- I'm sorry that I slammed the car door on your neck.

- Great! Someone just hacked into my pants.

- If you are not familiar with the proper ordering etiquette at a coffee stand and you need to dredge through that line of death, to somehow try to manage your way through an order that your loved one ever so politely asked you to go get for them, then that whole process will be as confusing as Steve Buscemi's teeth.
For Example;
Double ristretto, venti half soy, fair trade, nonfat, decaf, chocolate brownie, free range, organic, iced, one pump, sugar free, high gravity, gingerbread, caramel drizzle, pumpkin spice, whipped cream upside down, double blended, triple export, one sweet n' low, one-half regular NutraSweet, with ice, and Techron.
I have no damn idea what any of that means but it sure looks like a "recipe" in the Anarchists Cookbook.

- Speaking of The Price Is Right, what the hell was up with Bob Barker's microphone? Seriously, that thing was just a two-foot Slurpee straw with a small super ball at the end.

- Yanni = Yawny

- It's our ninth annual Yellow Tag Sale here at Warehouse Galleria Mart. Come in today for massive savings. You can't afford to miss this one; it's just that simple, come in and save.
We have easy financing and our friendly well-trained staff are dedicated to making sure you have a great shopping experience. Come in now for Warehouse Galleria Mart's Yellow Tag Sale.
We are open seven days a week from 8 AM to 10 PM, and we're conveniently located right across from the Taco Hut on 53rd & 3rd.
Come in now for our Yellow Tag Sale, where every one of our yellow tags are on sale.

- Not many people know this but the Grim Reaper only has one testicle.

- Don't be afraid of change. Change is good for you, except when you swallow it or get it stuck in your nose.

- One of my favorite songs from the 70's is *Driver's Seat* by Sniff and the Tears. I can't help but to think if you sniff the driver's seat, there will definitely be tears.

- Shotgun weddings have been around for ages, but Kurt and Courtney popularized the shotgun divorce.

- I am trying to sell the idea of a stage presentation to tour in Japan.
It's about an overweight single father who is raising his little son all alone, it's called "Fat Man and Little Boy."

- Am I the only one that hates that blueberry pancake bitch in Pulp Fiction?

- Anal cavities are caused by shoving candy bars and soda up your ass. Oh! And not brushing.

- There's nothing like seeing hungover sorority girls sifting through their vomit in the hopes of finding and retaking their undissolved morning after pill.
But on the other hand, that is a whole lot better than seeing hungover sorority girls sifting through someone else's vomit in the hopes of finding and taking *their* morning after pill.

4

Mr. Mean Buys a 6-Pack

- West Coast Mimes will hold a silent auction to raise money to help fund the Stuttering Foundation.

- Two stories side-by-side in yesterday's newspaper.
1) Kansas City Royal's second baseman Bernie Johansson denies allegations that he took performance enhancing drugs.
2) Teen Saved: Major League Baseball's Bernie Johansson saved an accident victim by lifting a car off of a trapped teenager.

- I find it ironic, yet a little humorous, that one of the largest retail chains in the U.S. aptly named *Target* was hit by a major credit card breach during the Black Friday weekend of 2013.

- Speaking of prison, I guess tossing some huge hairy dude's salad can only be taken as tongue-in-cheek.

- I would not like to visit the Ear Wax Museum.

- I don't know about you, but when I'm in a restaurant, the mere thought of my food being prepared "with love" absolutely disgusts me. I've heard enough horror stories about ticked off fast food restaurant employee's preparing food with "love."
"Order number 79! Double Cheeseburger with *special* sauce!"
No Way! Keep the love away from my meal.

- In the unlikely event of an emergency landing, your seat cushion may be used as a flotation device, or more likely it will be used as a wonderful little personal space to physically express your total utter fear of dying by soaking it with warm body fluids and excrement.

- Good news for job seekers! There's an *opening* at the OB/GYN clinic.

- I'm ready for pitching practice, I brought my ball bag.

- Do you have poopy thoughts?
Have you recently had sleep temptations?
Do you like French toast with lots of butter?
Do you have a fear of dying when you're getting beat to death by six large alpha males?
Does diarrhea run in your family?
Do you feel the need to wear a t-shirt with a wolf howling at the moon on it that you can only purchase at a country road gas station/truck stop?
If you answered yes or no to any of these questions then you quite possibly may or may not be suffering from something or other.

- I like how New Yorker's have turned the word "whore" into a two-syllable word. Seriously, It's pretty cool. "who-were."

- If you can see a seagull's butthole, then you are absolutely without a doubt in the wrong place.

- Business tip #17:
If you are planning on starting a summer camp that is structured around teaching children better focus skills and learning techniques. Do not! I repeat, DO NOT call it "Concentration Camp."

- Magnum 3.14

- The best thing about morons taking selfies together is that it greatly increases the chance of them spreading lice to each other.

- Ya gotta love gas station chili that is served from a pump.

- In the fine print of the back of a state lottery ticket, it states that "persons altering tickets are subject to criminal prosecution." Just to fuck with them, I will hem those tickets, or maybe add an inseam, and if I'm really in the mood, I will throw a couple of buttons on it.
There's your altered ticket.

- I never have liked the song Funk #49 by the James Gang, I sure hope that #50 or #51 is better.

- An upside-down boob is poop.

- Here is a fun trick to play on some guy. He will need a couple of one-dollar bills. Have the poor sap hold a dollar bill in each hand and have him count to ten. Now, right when he gets to three, kick him really hard right in the nuts. If you kick him hard enough, you should see vomit. Then, while he is lying on the ground crying and retching, take his two dollars and go buy yourself a Dr. Pepper.

- I will reveal a secret shortly.

- As a repeat winner of the largest pumpkin contest on my half of the street I live on, I will now share with you what I use to grow such mammoth pumpkins. I grow them in a three-part fertile soil and one-part shredded documents from the Pentagon mixture.

- I just revealed a secret.

- Have you ever noticed anytime you are beating somebody over the head repeatedly with a golf club, it seems to be at this exact moment when you remember that you forgot to go to the grocery store to pick up fresh vegetables for a dinner salad?

- I have nothing against really old folks, but I have to say, kicking their walkers and canes out from under them is fun as hell. I once even got two of them on the ground with a single swipe of my foot.

- I like to make big cement balls in the shape of balloons, then paint them a bright color and tie a three foot ribbon onto it. Then when nobody is looking I gently lay it in the middle of the street.

- Remember this commercial from the 70's and 80's?

"4 out of 5 dentists recommend Trident gum?" Well, what they didn't tell us is, the actual survey that was given to just over 3,600 dentists that belong to the American Dental Association was as follows...

"What would you rather chew on?"

1. Easter Peeps
2. A table leg
3. Trident Gum
4. Cat turds

- I am not sure what lead up to this but Siri just challenged me to a fight behind the portables during recess.

5

Root Up!

- Funk #98 is twice as better of a song as Funk #49.

- When I go out, I like to go out with a bang. That's why after I lock my front door when I leave the house, I light a couple of M-80's on my porch.

- Let's get this straight - when all of the air leaks out of your tire from when you take a short cut through someone's yard and take out their ultra-hydro 3000 titanium sprinkler, or when the femur bone from your neighbor's dog punctures it, it is not, I repeat, it is not a flat tire! It is what you would call a non-circular tire.

"Oh crap Dave! You just ran over that dude in a wheelchair! Pull this hunk of shit over; you have a non-circular tire."

A flat tire is when you melt that bitch down to a liquid form and pour it onto your driveway.

- Ahhh, gas station grotesqueries, the quickest route to heartburn and effervescent flatulence.

- Speaking of stained sheets, Martha Stewart, the Duchess of Drapes, the Lady of Linen, the Freak of Fondue, the Queen of Craft, has had a very successful career with many lasting accomplishments; a magazine publication called "Martha Stewart Living" being one of them.

Martha was born in 1941 which makes her about, oh, a thousand years old. Statistically speaking, little Ms. Cookiesheet will set her table for the last time and will be shopping at that big craft store in the sky in the near future. With that being said, she should seriously consider changing the name of her publication as soon as possible. Martha Stewart Living is not going to fly when she's deceased. As a matter of fact, that would be a downright lie.

That's the kind of thing I think of when I'm dealing with compressed turkey logs the day after Thanksgiving.

- I saw a sign that read "BURN BAN IN PLACE."
Now that's not very specific, there is a whole crap load of places, as a matter of fact, there is millions upon millions of places. Which place is that sign referring to?

- When is someone going to make a men's cologne that smells like WD40? I could get behind that.

- Bea Arthur or be dead.

- Do animals pulverized by a shotgun blast count as mechanically separated?

- I would love to see a game show, where the contestant has to choose a brick out of a little pyramid, in which that brick will be set aside and used later in the game as a wild card. Then later in the show, right after the loser round, he/she beats the living daylights out of the host with the wild card.

- Lice: the other white crabs.

- Hunting the North American Bovinian can be a challenging hobby. Locating one is the easy part; it's luring them away from their habitat that can be the dangerous part.
The North American Bovinian is often found in casinos and buffet restaurants everywhere, often perched in a state of sedation in front of a slot machine or grazing angrily at the buffet.
The most successful way to remove them from said location is with bribery. I find that a trail of Hershey's Kisses or quarters will work every time. Once they have rolled out of the building you can now trap them for easy removal or just tag them and let them back into the wild.

- Every sock I own has a hole in it, some of them even have more than one. As a matter of fact, every sock on this planet has at least one hole in it.
Get it? Please don't make me explain.

- Have you ever attended any kind of gathering where they served fruit punch? Isn't that just disgusting? Especially if it's served in a swimming pool sized punch bowl - by the end of the event, there will be a half an inch of unwanted, diseased, sediment at the bottom, you know... fecal matter, scabs, rings, dry skin, boogers, band-aids, and anything else that may slide off your hands.
I've never liked it, and never will. I don't even like the name...Fruit Punch, sounds like a hate crime.

- The toxicology report states that Led Zeppelin drummer, John Bonham, died from having too much led in his blood.
That's the kind of thing I think of when I'm dealing a pair of deuces and a flush in bathroom poker.

- Kurt Cobain's toxicology report states that he died from too much lead in his system as well. Hey! Don't yell at me, I'm just stating the facts folks.

- Have you ever woken up your dog because you think it's having a bad dream? It's sleeping away like the little asshole it is and all of a sudden, it starts "sleep barking" and twitching. Well, who the hell are we to play the peacemaker? Poor little Daisy was probably having a wonderful dream of having a three-way with Clifford and Marmaduke. Let sleeping dogs lie.

- Dang it! I just spilled Big Mac sauce on my yoga mat, *again*.

- Have you ever noticed that the countries against abortions, birth control, and homosexuality are the ones that have certain groups of alpha-male ass wipes that single handedly kill the most innocent people strictly based on a difference in beliefs?

- Hey ladies! Having trouble getting pregnant? Move into a trailer; you're guaranteed to pound out six kids in four and a half years.

- As soon as "Insta-Death" comes in an aerosol can, I'm going to pick up a dozen. There's a few child eating dogs on my mail route that need to be eliminated.

- Time for me to snivel. This one was written while delivering the mail in a blistering 98-degree day. The next person that comes out of their air-conditioned home and says, "Is it hot enough for you?" without offering me a cold bottle of water is getting cup-checked by a size twelve postal work boot.

- Thank you for watching the 700 Club today where we discussed the tragic loss of nine key members of our 700 Club team in a bowling accident last Thursday. Please tune in next week to the 691 Club.

- I am sure there is a blues artist out there somewhere with the name Fat Johnson.

- I'm a man who likes to plan ahead. I like to be ready for any situation that may present itself. For instance, when I go mountain climbing, I like to have my climbing partners, Reuben, Patty, and Alfredo with me, that way if I am in a dire situation and trapped for a long period of time, I wouldn't feel so bad about eating them.

- My idea of hole foods - donuts, bagels, Swiss cheese, and Cheerios.

- Wallace G. Henderson, the owner of the Pantomime Theater in New York city died April 17th, 1937 from head injuries he received while brushing his teeth. He was crowned the king of silent comedy in 1928, where he went on to win many awards in the art of mime. Over four-hundred people attended his funeral where nobody said shit the entire time - you know, as a tribute.

- What's another name for thesaurus?

- When hanging out backstage and whooping it up with other artists at the Austin Blues Festival, the conversation eventually led to "touring benefits." Naturally as these are musicians, the subject of benefits led to the question of "How many times they had sex while on tour." That is precisely the exact moment when 5' 4" bluesman Tiny Johnson realized he chose the wrong stage name.

- This is March, so do you know what the means folks? It is Colon Cancer Awareness Month. You will notice a crap load more pictures of Tom Cruise in the media because what else reminds us of a colon more than good ol' Tom.

- Marshall, Will, and Holly are the O.G. cave dwellers.
#landofthelost

6

Love, Rain, and the Nestucca Spit Kelp Factor

- We are living in an "ask your doctor if" society.

That's where we, the public consumer, are influenced by commercials, advertisements, and the media about what chronic life ending diseases these ads suggest we have.

Let's face it, if you "decide" you have something wrong with you based on a commercial or advertisement, then you may be a perfect candidate for some of these side effects that come with those little happy pills, like:

Nausea, drowsiness, insomnia, vomiting, dry mouth, effervescent flatulence, headaches, crunchy scrotum, numbness in arms or legs, hives, blood in stool, caustic snot, hyper pungency, sparking stool, diarrhea, mental or mood changes, irritability, impulsive urethral trajectories, muscle twitching, itchy dick, herniated shadow, interior hair, swelling of feet, swelling of teeth, puffy retinas, false sense of well-being, oscillating testes, epidermal lactation, chronic post coital forked urine stream (C.P.C.F.U.S.), thin drizzling shits, Stevie Nicks Voice, abscessed nipples, shitbreath,

continued...........

loss of appetite, loss of memory, loss of keys, nightmares, nightmares of losing your keys, nightmares of nightmares, bronchial oxidation, intestinal purging, popcorn farts, seven year itch, twelve year rash, octo-crotch, cloudy or bloody urine, abnormal vision, bloody vision, squishy feet, testicular palsy, illusions of enlightenment, massive nostrils, doughnut hole, dry eyes, dry mouth, dry hole, flushing, clogging, plunging, hair pain, elongated thoughts, thoughts of elongation, rectal bleeding, sores on the mouth, scabs on the rod, lopsided kidneys, astro-labia, the sniffles, papilla strain, anal Tourette's, perforated sack, George Thorogood mouth, rotten crotch, open sores, worms, ear paralysis, farmers lung, inverted penis, perverted penis, Siamese penis, external vagina, whipper snapper, bowlers itch, restless neck syndrome, faucet booty, flaccidness, jetting jib, eye cankers, liver acne, hyper caustic semen, fuzzy tongue, tracheal discharge, shitty nodules, finger erections, labial carnage, escalating socket, ovary oozing,

continued...........

bowlers balls, masticating mucous syndrome, penis farts, worms, refined calcium deposits, protruding satchel, concave brow ridge, neck nut, biker's crotch, lotus gait, dirty salad trots, low I.Q. - high B.O., webbed tongue, funnel vision, speckled penis, ulcerated collarbones, gangrene colon, twitching vulva, truckers ass, dehydrated hymen, baboon butt, vulvalatory projections, taco cock, massive flaccid ass, the crabs, the scorpions, corn cob in the stool, retracted bladder, cervical searing, mangled gums, hyper extended birth canal, womb rot, squatters knob, seepage, genital static, imploding uterus, swimmers crotch, fractured psyche, orange teeth, tangled vocal cords, herniated hemorrhoids, inapt pelvis, mad yeast rising, alien jaw, urethral atrophy, spontaneous pregnancy, bowel engorgement, joo-joo eyeball, monkey finger, walrus gumboot, spinal cracker, mojo filter, micro-soft, thunder finger, loss of mammaries, asshole blowout, deviated rectum, demonic scalp, trans vaginal mesh, potty mouth, potty breath, potty face, afro-cock,

continued...........

crotch crickets, dispersed knuckles, bio-fist, the blues, yellow fever, black plague, blue balls, scarlet fever, pink eye, black death, yellow jaundice, and bright navy blue influenza.

-   I'd rather lather, than gather splatter matter.

-   For some reason I can't explain, I hope that Tonya Harding and Bobby Brown are both sitting in an empty room and crying right now. Not together of course, that would be weird.

-   Sometimes you just gotta lean to the side and let one rip.

-   Every coat is a coat of arms, unless if it is a vest. Is a vest even a coat?

- Have you noticed an influx of restaurants that offer gluten for free? It's pretty easy to tell because they usually have a sign in the window that says "GLUTEN FREE." Great idea but bad grammar. Furthermore, is it any coincidence that some of those same restaurants also offer Range Chicken for free as well. Maybe they should advertise, "Free Range Chicken and Gluten!" Okay, that seemed funnier in my head.
Dear editor, please edit this out.
Dear Stan, kiss my ass, sincerely, your editor.

- This book is definitely not gluten free. I have put so much gluten into this book, each word is slathered in gluten. Every individual page is drizzled with gluten. The whole damn book is marinated in gluten. After reading this book you will feel as though you were just sucker punched with the giant sticky fist from the God of Gluten.

- Do blind people "dot" their eyes?

- I am not a fan of spooning, I'm more of a melon balling kind of guy. Get it?

- Sad news, the creator of the excavator has passed away at the age of 94. Richard Abernethy was buried in his hometown of Lloyd, Alabama where this small town of 8,500 residents paid tribute to Richard by digging him up with a caterpillar 345CL Excavator.

- The Ultimate Zen: The deepest state of meditation, often resulting in a complete and total unresponsiveness to your surroundings and a slight probability that you may scorch your shorts.

- The average "all-you-can-eat-buffet" abuser will use approximately fifty-seven Western Hemlocks, thirty-eight Noble Firs, and one Sitka Spruce cleaning their assholes in their lifetime.

- I Dream of Genealogy

- Sigmund Freud once said "sometimes a cigar is just a cigar." Well I say "a stupid person with a smart phone is still a stupid person."
Yeah, I know those two quotes have nothing to do with each other.

- I'm like a pain relief ointment, I'm fast acting, deep penetrating, and I smell minty.

- I do not understand why the person at a restaurant that takes your order is called a waiter or waitress, shouldn't a customer be called a waiter? Isn't that what we are doing? Waiting? Waiting to be seated. Waiting to place our order. Waiting for our food. Waiting for the bill. Customers = Waiters

INTER

MISSION

7

Whoop a Clown

- There are approximately 153,424.7 deaths per day on this planet, so If I did the math correctly, 14.4 people just died as you were reading this bit.

- I just finished writing an entire concept album called 2113. It's just like 2112 by Rush, but one better.

- I blame Bruce Springsteen.

- Never submit a destination address into your GPS using your voice while the radio is on. No sooner than when I got onto the highway it said "now drive straight down for 6,278 miles."
I then remembered *Highway to Hell* by AC/DC was on the radio at the time.

- Stevie Wonder Boy George Michael Jackson Brown

- Gland sanitizer sells well in Las Vegas.

- I always wondered what would happen if you gave Viagra to a snake - "Holy Moses, it turned into a walking staff!"

- Triglycerides? I don't even know what a glyceride it, so why would I want to try one?

- Time to start eating better. I just cut myself and mozzarella and Red Bull came oozing out.

- Speaking of voice text, just for shits and giggles I farted into my phone and it displayed the word "enchilada."

- I still blame Bruce Springsteen.

- My two stupid dogs humped before I had them fixed. To make matters worse, little Chica had Lyme Disease and Rico had Lemon Disease. Guess what? Little Chica gave birth to a can of Sprite.

- Ahhhhh, lunch AND dinner at Taco Hut. I now have a horn section backing me up that is so loud it would knock Tower of Power right out of the box.

- Does your I.Q. Score automatically diminish by four when you get all your wisdom teeth removed?

- Is it wrong that I smile when I see a very large dog resembling a small tour bus drop a steaming triple coiler on a perfectly manicured lawn?

- In the past seventy-two hours, my stoolabatory output volume has surpassed my ingesticated input level. Trust me, I did the math.
$M(in) - M(out) = dM/dT.$

- S.C.A.L.P.
Sioux Civilization and Land Preservation

- My ass has Tourettes.

- Somewhere, (probably West Virginia) there is a dude smoking pot in his *high* chair.

- Jefferson Airplane: the acid years.
Jefferson Starship: the drunk and fighting years.
Starship: the hairspray and video years.
Jefferson Cruiseship: the casino and walker years.

- I'm really getting tired of all of these pop singers, or as I like to refer to them, "trust fund baby artists."

- The following idea may have already been implemented but I have no way of knowing. I think the men's and women's crappers in church should be labeled as hymns and hyrs.

- Let's play a game, I don't have a name for it yet so we will just call it "Give Me Twenty Dollars." You go first.

\-   Speaking of cannibals, what's good on the menu here at Fleshington's Fine Human Cuisine?

Well, today's special is our fajita style scalp wrap made with mechanically separated kid, diced interior cartilage, and seared labia, lightly drizzled with a spicy bile duct excretory sauce.

Hook that up with a basket of hot fetal fries, throw in a brain jelly smoothie, and you have yourself a tasty treat that's fun to eat.

Don't forget about our happy hour menu which includes our famous $5.99 battered face quesadillas, or savory handburgers served on a toasted ass-bun. Also, coming next summer, we will please you noodle nuts with our raw-man noodle bar.

\-   If the Red Hot Chili Peppers, Goo Goo Dolls, and Godsmack never existed, EVERYTHING would be just a little bit better.

- There is an actual disease called "beaver fever." Look it up.

- Damn you, automatic data validation function! I only wanted to look up *Louisiana Meat Rub*, not *Wheezy Anna Meat Rub*. That's what I get for using voice text. Oh, how I wish I could unsee what I just saw.

- If you were in a fight with a clown and he had you in a headlock, wouldn't you have the urge to reach back and honk his nose?

- How come we have never seen one of those goofy colorful bicycle shirts with this printed on the back?
"Don't *tread* on me"
Speaking of inconsiderate one-hundred-fifteen-pound lane hogs, here's a saying that I would like to implement into reality.
"I share bicycles with the road." Think about that one for a bit.

- I don't find it necessary to give any effort to save someone that is choking on a plumb-bob.

- Isn't the last few squirts of ketchup fun? The way that plastic container farts is always a table pleaser.

- Did you know that in Punta Gorda, Florida, steam is against the law?

- Do you want to see something funny? Starve a man for three days - he can only have four ounces of water per day - and then give him ten pounds of extra salted peanuts.

- How far into something do you have to be before you drop your shorts and sing *Yellow Submarine*?

- Face the facts people, *Back in Black* by AC/DC is the most successful rap song ever recorded.

- I had a fly land on my hand yesterday, so I waved my arm around in a spastic manner to let the little bugger experience what it is like to ride a roller coaster. I'd sure want a giant to do the same for me.

- Speaking of 70's and 80's music, if I was a long-haul truck driver, I would surely like to be *haulin' oats*. See where I went with that?

- I was flipping through the channels and settled on *The Golden Girls Reunion Special*. It wasn't bad at all, except about half way through the program, I realized I was actually watching *The Walking Dead*. I should've known something was up when what appeared to be the cute short lady was walking along minding her own business when some dipshit on a motorcycle shot an arrow through her face.

- Thespacebaronmycomputerisbroken.

- Great,

now

my

space   bar

is

sticking.

- Here are a couple of advertising bits
that never saw the light of day.
"Hi! I'm Kurt Cobain for Mr. Pibb. If
you're going to take a shit load of drugs,
why not wash them down with a
delicious ice cold Mr. Pibb?"
"Hello, I'm Samuel L. Jackson for
broccoli. Fuck celery!"

8

A Glowing Urethra Bolt

- I guess the people involved with naming New York, New Hampshire, New Jersey, and New Mexico, didn't have longevity in mind.
It's been well over a couple of centuries now; there is absolutely nothing new about those states anymore.

- I was asked "what's your favorite beer?" Well, the answer is quite simple. It's the one that is closest to me.

- I'm thinking big here. My next book will be "live." You read it as I write it. It will be about ten months long with a shit load of mistakes.

- I have a rotary dial cell phone.

- Now in sports! The Cleveland Eagles beat the holy fucking hell out of the West Seattle Wildcats in what was a complete humiliating annihilation for West Seattle with a score of 3-2.
Back to you Jane!

- What do you think of when I say "Timmy is blowing bubbles?"
Now, what do you think of when I say "Michael Jackson is blowing Bubbles?"
Let me clarify something here. Mr. Fancy-pants Jackson had a pet monkey named Bubbles.
See where I went with that?

- No really! Where have all the cowboys gone?

- The company that makes "Pam No-Stick Cooking Spray" has merged with the "Scotch Brand Scotch Tape" company to make "Scam: No-Stick Tape."

- I literally just farted the first four notes of *Purple Haze* by Jimi Hendrix.

- Why is it that so many stores around December have a "urine closeout sale?"

-    We have Chief Meteorologist Jane Buttswipe with the weather.

"Thank you Dick! Today we have a 90% chance of shitty sun, with clouds rolling in around 10:00 tonight, and for tomorrow, we're looking at a 100% chance of beautiful rain with isolated thundershowers."

Isolated? Bullshit! What the hell is an "isolated thundershower?"

Here's an isolated thundershower for you. "Tonight, we'll have a butt load of rain with thunder that only Steve Johnson will hear on his way to buy more crack."

Back to you Dick!

-    Either somebody just drunk texted me or there's a person in Kazakhstan that is telling me to piss off. The text reads "ha sexy, eat my pig."

-    Did you know that if you stare at a clock long enough, you'll eventually die? I mean, you would have to stare at it for a really, really, really, long time.

- Doesn't the map of South America look like a fucked up, crooked, double scoop ice cream cone with approximately 30% of one of the scoops licked away?
Alright! Alright. I know it's far-fetched, but dang it, let's see you come up with a more idiotic but yet fairly accurate comparison.

- Great news! I'm finally finished with my book, "How To Pay Off Your House in 30 Days."
The release date is July 9th. Pre-order through June 23rd for a special low price of $217,695 and receive a wonderful bookmark.

- Let me go on record here, I do not get out of the shower to pee.

- Word

- Four out of five dentists recommend Trident gum, the remaining 20% recommend soda and caramels.

- I just wanted to include the word "brucellosis" in this book. That's all.

Hey! Why not? Does your book contain the word brucellosis? I didn't think so.

As far as I can tell, this is the only book written in my neighborhood that has the word brucellosis in it.

Oh, by the way, while we're on the subject, brucellosis is also known as "Contagious Abortion" or "Bang's Disease." For real, look it up.

- Products that might not sell well #86
  - Colonic mouthwash
  - Electric gargler
  - Cactus Patch Kids
  - Tickle Me Phil Anselmo doll
  - Sour cream flavored tooth paste
  - Automatic "she loves me/she loves me not" petal picker
  - Fly strip / potato peeler combo
  - Home fire alarm with sixteen soothing ambient sounds

- I used to be a heavy drinker, until I lost forty-five pounds. Now I'm just an average weight drinker.

- If a deaf person who communicates with sign language has two fingers in a cast, would that be considered poor grammar? Just wondering.

- Speaking of SAT scores, I live in a city where the #1 stolen item is the grocery store shopping cart. No lie.

- Whenever I am troubled and feel I have the weight of the world on my shoulders, I just stop what I'm doing, take a nice long hike through Mother Nature's majestic beauty.........and chop down a big ass tree.

- "It was a dark and stormy night........." Damn it, Snoopy! You've had us all hanging in suspense for all these years, please finish the damn story already.

- Dick Dorkin suffered severe injuries to his spine from attempting to open a ketchup packet with greasy fingers.

-    Corn: Nature's tracer.
Eat it and start the clock.

-    Astronomer Ulopf Sak Pylvinian's
two-year push to make his 2010 discovery
of a very distant star constellation
official, has been completely grounded
by the Astronomy & Space Science
Research Center. What was believed to
be a six-star constellation approximately
180,000 light years beyond the Orion's
Belt was nothing more than Ulopf's eye
floaters.

-    Buy one and get one free! You buy
one and I get the free one.

-    I wonder how many vehicle accidents
are due to having explosive diarrhea?

-    Have you ever seen that rainbow-
colored crud on packaged lunch meat?
What is that?

9

James! That Went Out.....

- Monkey's:
Elvis had a porcelain monkey.
The Beastie Boys had brass monkey.
Mick Jagger is a monkey man.
Peter Gabriel shocked the monkey.
Warren Zevon said "leave my monkey alone."
The Beatles claimed that "everybody's got something to hide except me and my monkey."
Finally, the Monkees declared they were the Monkees and that they monkey around.
Enough with the monkeys already! Its overkill. Can't people just sing about giraffes or penguins?

- Tony Chin - ya gotta respect a man named after three different parts of the body.

- After your vasectomy, there will be a vast difference in your vas deferens.

- When you're in a rush while pounding one out and your steamer is just chillin,' hanging there like a sleeping bat, you will need to decrapitate that thing.

- Have you ever watched "the Golden Girls" and realized that you had a hard-on? No? Oh....um. OK, so, how about them Seahawks?

- Now picture this, I have a picture of a pitcher drinking a pitcher of beer in Picher, Oklahoma.

- Here's a no-no often done by men in their upper 50's that are trying to recapture the vitality of their youth. They dye their thinning grey hair a color so dark it can only be described as *evil black*, which looks absolutely awful, and should really be called Scalp Highlighter.

- Bill Cosby's sweaters that he wore on *The Cosby Show* look like something a cartoonist threw up.

- This is just five words.

- Here's just one of the many things wrong with the United States - check this advertisement out.

"Now at Burger Death! The Massive Big Death Sexy Combo Meal! Say Hello to our famous two-and-a-half-pound bacon and cream cheese burger on our mouthwatering savory fried butter doughnut bun. Hook that up with a jaw dropping super-duper god damned mondo triple basket of fried Death Fries and wash it all down with a delicious quad chocolate eggnog thirty-two ouncer Death Shake.

All for only $2.49 at participating Burger Death Restaurants.

(*Here's the fast-talking part of the commercial*)

Burger Death is a L.L.C. Burger Death is not responsible for any strokes, cardiac arrests, criminal arrests, deaths, choking, or......*(etc, etc)*

It's no wonder the U.S. is the sweatpants capital of the world.

- Some people call me Maurice.

- In all reality, "afternoon" is actually twenty-three hours, fifty-nine minutes, and fifty-nine seconds long, which works out great for me because I'm more of an afternoon person.

- Thank you for reading this sentence.

- They say if you hold a large shell up to your ear you can hear the ocean. In South Chicago, if you hold a gang member up to your ear you can hear him shoot you.

- I just quit cold turkey. From now on, I heat that shit up.

- Zamfir: Master of the Pan Flute, ain't got shit on Bobby: Master of the Ladle Flute.

- I should shit in Cheryl's She-Shed.

\-   "Several months ago, I became a father for the very first time."

-J. Foxworthy

Listen up doofus! You can only become a father once, and from that point on, you are always a father.

"You might be a butthole redneck if you become a father for the first time, twice."

-S. Nelson

\-   Have you heard any songs from Lyle Lovett and his Very Large Head Band? I haven't.

\-   If you are experiencing dry and itchy eyes, then you may have dry and itchy eyes. That's the kind of thing I think of when I'm streaming a #1 and downloading a #2 while in the bathroom.

- It's well-known rock lore that when Iron Butterfly singer Doug Ingle was in the studio recording their seventeen-minute classic *In-A-Gadda-Da-Vida*, he was so drunk that he couldn't even sing the original penned title of the song which was supposed to be "In the Garden of Eden."

In a similar, but not as well-known story, Simon and Garfunkel's *Bridge Over Troubled Water* was born from that exact situation.

Art Garfunkel was on day six of a whiskey and PCP bender when he had to be wheeled into the studio to do some vocal tracks. Art was unable to read the lyric sheet or even speak. With the deadline looming, Simon and Garfunkel had to release what he incoherently sang that night.

Paul Simon said in a recent interview, "Things were never the same after that, Art completely destroyed the song, he sang like shit and sounded awful. He was totally incomprehensible, but we were out of time, so we had to use that vocal track. I mean, he couldn't even get the title of the song correctly, he actually

continued...........

sang it as 'bridge over troubled water.'
What kind of dip shit would sing that?
What does that even mean? It was
supposed to be "hamburger apple fly
swatter." He destroyed the band with
that stunt."

- There's a new over-the-counter
medicine for people addicted to stealing
shit. Clepto-Bismol.

- Dick asks Bob a question about an
insect.
"Hey Bob, what kind of bug is this?
That's a tick Dick, as a matter of fact,
that's a tick from a dik-dik Dick, and be
careful because you can get sick by a
prick of a tick from a dik-dik Dick, trust
me, you never want to get sick by a prick
from the tick of a dik-dik Dick. Rick got
sick by a prick of a tick from a dik-dik
Dick, and do you know what happened
to Rick when he got sick by a prick of a
tick from a dik-dik Dick? Rick died."

- I'm just throwing this out there. I feel it's perfectly fine to have a billboard sign advertising movies like "The Terminator" directly in front of an abortion clinic.

- The only thing I don't like about rain is that it dilutes my beer when I'm drinking outdoors.

- I didn't have much money while growing up, so I took my favorite sport out of the alley and into the playground. It was back then that I relentlessly practiced bowling against a brick wall.

- Two pairs of pears are half of a pie. I really don't know why that was written in my notes for this book. I was going to leave it out, but it is so stupid I thought I'd throw it in here. Just keeping it real.

- In a nineteen-year study at Hosen University, scientists have determined that wearing your pants in a low-rider sag style will make it 82.139% more difficult to run from authorities.

- Rap artist Sean "P. Diddy" Combs has changed his name so many times he's giving John Mellencamp a run for his money.
The latest count so far is:

Sean Combs - 8
John Mellencamp – 5

Eventually they will morph into the same artist and become Sean Mellencamp. Here's a crazy idea, use your damn birth name.

- Hitchhikers are some of the nicest people you will even see. Every time I pass one up they let me know I'm doing a good job.

10

Beat Up a Tree

- I can't figure out how to use "the selfish shellfish" in a sentence.

- Here's something that really stinks. So, you're driving to the clinic to pick up some more cream for your rash and you suddenly smell something that resembles burning metal and wires. You're sure that it's your vehicle and it is going to go up in flames any second. So, now you are violently sniffing the air in panic mode, in hopes that the stink subsides, so you will be assured that it is not your piece of shit vehicle that is releasing that stank. Meanwhile, from all the extreme sniffing you have given yourself a massive head rush that's so bad you've entered a state of vertigo that only Bono can describe in a song. Then you crash into the back of a propane truck which erupts into a volcanic fireball and you die.

- If I'm introduced to somebody and they let me know within twenty seconds into the conversation that they are college educated, I instantly categorize them under "loser" in my asshole files.

- Prostitution as a *hole*, really isn't all that bad.

- Let's talk about lacrosse for a moment. Yeah, you know, that sport where upper class white teens and young adults run around in expensive gear and try to catch a rubber ball in a mesh athletic protective cup on the end of a broom handle. That's all, the moment is over, I don't want to talk about it anymore.

- I actually do know Jack Squat. I went to school with him in the ninth grade.

- Is the word dictionary in the dictionary? Would you actually open up the book to look it up? Think about it - it's right there on the cover.

- The inside of the door to the Pancake Corral in Bellevue, Washington is quite possibly the stickiest object in the known universe. Even stickier than the inside of Motley Crue's tour bus.

- I have a patent on "the wedgie." Every time some unlucky kid receives one, I get four cents.

- I want one of those 793 foot motor homes with a painting of a bobcat stalking and ready to strike on the back of it.
No wait! Forget the bobcat, I want the painting to be a silhouette of a naked woman in an uncomfortable position.
No wait! Forget the naked woman, I want a magical sorcerer or wizard with electricity shooting out of his wand and a crystal ball with lots of lightning everywhere.
No wait! Forget the magical sorcerer, I want a nature scene consisting of a lake with a huge snowcapped mountain looming in the near distance with an eagle flying overhead.
No wait! Forget the mountain, I want a large map of the United States and I'll fill in all of the states I've been in.
Oh never mind, I couldn't possibly afford one of those motor homes anyways, I'll just put a "RUSH" bumper sticker on my old truck.

- When hitchhiking, you must follow the one rule of thumb.

- So, I found out that I can work my anus with such precision that I can tie two turds together. I shit you knot!

- Is it a success or a failure if attendance at the marijuana anonymous meetings has been very high? I'm just wondering.

- There is no better name for a deceased artist than Drew.

- The best thing about a fast food kid's meal is that the toy is more nutritious than the meal.

- If dogs ceased to exist, I would still manage to somehow step in a big steaming pile of dog crap.

- I like to sing Motorhead songs during my shower. The shower head way up in the cradle makes the perfect "Lemmy" microphone.

- I'm glad I don't smoke pot, I just have a feeling that I wouldn't handle seeing "Jack" from the Jack In The Box commercials very well. That huge perfectly round head with a monstrous smile and an extra creepy hat that is constantly about to fall off. I think I would lose my shit and run out the door.

- International House of Pain Pancakes.

- The Bulimia Awareness Foundation is holding its annual "Party Til' You Puke" potluck this Sunday at the Red Lion Inn. A main food dish and a donation of at least one hundred dollars is required for admittance. Come get your puke on at this white carpet event. There will also be clowns to help with the purging - you know, because it's easier to hurl when you're looking at a clown. Scrunchies and Tic-Tac's will be handed out at the door.

- As you may have heard, it rains a butt load here in the Seattle area. With that being said, When I pick up my dumb dogs crap in the back yard, I notice that those little disgusting mounds of hatred look like "fluffy dung sponges." You may ask, what is a "fluffy dung sponge?"
Well, a "fluffy dung sponge" is what your dog's crap looks like in your back yard after 26 consecutive days of rain in the Seattle area.

- Dandelions are like lazy dudes, they are irritating, indolent, and they don't do shit except spread their seed all over the place, thus producing more unwanted dandelions.

- In the name of prognostication, I sincerely hope that Billy Squire never has a stroke. On the other hand, the extreme irony if he were to have one would make for great banter.

- Anal warts are caused by shoving angry frogs up your ass.

- I'm just throwing this out there - What if there was an annual music festival in Jackson Hole, Wyoming headlined by Jackson Brown? That's all, I don't have anything witty about this. Because I don't think "Brown-Hole Palooza" is funny.

- I put Crazy Glue in your Crazy Straw.

11

I Saw a Cat Named Ray from the Bus on 49th Ave.

- There's something humorous about seeing man or woman in a nice suit performing a "farmer's blow."

- Note to self: Do not roast hot dogs on an open fire while burning household items such as a VCR, shoes, and a rubber hose.

- I find irony in the fact that people are born on Labor Day.

- The first two lines in the song *Ruby Tuesday* are actually sung by Kermit the Frog.

- Thank you for flying Speed of Light Airlines, where we will be departing Sea-Tac Airport in just a few minutes. With the current weather, we will be arriving at London's Heathrow Airport last Tuesday. Let us remind you that if you have just recently screwed up something in your life, then we are your airline, so let us help you undo that shit you fucked-up with Speed of Light Airlines.

- Aging classic rock artist George Thorogood had a hit in the early 1990's called *I Drink Alone*. Within the song there are two lines that have bugged the crap out of me since the first time I heard it. The lines are:

"You know when I drink alone,
I prefer to be by myself."

Now I'm no linguist - as a matter of fact I would call myself the anti-linguist - but those two lines together makes as much sense as Keith Richards during an interview.

So, I say to George, "I think you drank too much."

- "Does this skirt make my wang look big?"

-Bruce/Caitlyn Jenner

- Sonny Bono was a tree hugger.

- You know you are in a cruddy neighborhood when the urine-stained mattresses by the side of the road are tagged with gang graffiti.

- I have a great idea for a reality show that could be a hit with the American Imbecile Society. Round up nine to ten major drug addicts, and no, I don't mean some idiot who claims he has a problem because he craves substance. I'm talking some hard-core rat eating, kill you for five dollars kind of guys. You know, the kind of freaks that puke up their stomach lining if they go eighteen hours without drinking gasoline. Now take these fine law-abiding citizens and throw them all in a large empty room that contains nothing but a massive pile of cocaine on the floor. Here's the fun part, you arm each idiot with only a plastic spork. Oh boy! There's nothing like fiendish addicts stabbing heads with broken sporks to attract millions of viewers. And check this out - it's the only show where the winner is also the loser. I call this show "Whose Line Is It Anyway?"

- Four forks for four dollars at the Four Winds Store in the Four Corners Plaza on Fourth and Forest in Forks, WA. Fuck yeah!

- I have an Apple iPod, a BlackBerry, ham radio, and I have cookies and spam on my PC. Now all I need is a Burrito Phone.

- The capitals of the United States of America are U.S.A. Just like the capital of Washington is W, or the capital of Texas is T, or the capital of North Dakota is N.D. Got it? You didn't think of that, I did, so there!

- An itchy crab probably has a case of the humans.

- Edward Scissor Hands: Beaver Cleaver Hands

- I just changed my mind. I don't do that very often but I just wasn't happy with the mind I had.

- Today is December 10th, but in reality, it's actually January 344th.

- Hi! I'm Brent Stevenson for the Hypohermaphofungaloculartitis-D Foundation, Hypohermaphofungaloculartitis-D has been a growing problem here in the U.S. for over five decades now. If you would like to help end Hypohermaphofungaloculartitis-D then please donate what you can to the Hypohermaphofungaloculartitis-D Foundation at www.Hypohermaphofungaloculartitis-D.org/hypohermaphofungaloculartitis-D. We thank you very much from the team at Hypohermaphofungaloculartitis-D.org/hypohermaphofungaloculartitis-D.

- Here's something you never see, a transient with a lint roller.

- Traffic in this city is so bad it can only be described as just like being stuck behind a ninety-year-old obese man doing a Chinese Fire drill.

- Regalia Rasputin von Hammer - if you meet this person, don't mess with him/her because that name alone can kick your ass into next December.

- Shouldn't a chef also be called a panhandler?

- There are over 7,000 generally utilized characters in modern Chinese language. That's one hell of a big ass can of alphabet soup.

- Every year after his annual fishing trip to Alaska, my friend Duke smokes some of the salmon he catches. Now I may not be the smartest cat in the litter but I am guessing that he's not going to catch any kind of buzz from that.

- Speaking of worldwide studies. I have single handedly raised the average times a human farts in a one day period by .004

- YouTube, iTunes, MySpace, Wii, and Minecraft, it's official, the youth of today are the "Personal Pronoun Generation."

- Forgive me if I seem a little irritated right now, but I was hoping to visit the labial district last night.

- If white people want to prove their diversity and unification principles, then I say they should change the names of Rodeo Drive and Hollywood Boulevard to Martin Luther King Jr. Way and Sitting Bull Drive.

- Am I the only person that finds if nearly impossible to call a man Dick? Now I don't mean calling a man a dick! I do that often; I can do that with ease. But to engage in a conversation with a man named Dick and actually call him Dick. I just can't do it, I've tried, but I always turn into Beavis and Butthead and start giggling uncontrollably.

- Now a word from our sponsor, "Yum-Yum Extra Strength Dishwater Detergent." It's time to beat the crap out of those stubborn filthy dishes. These individual detergent pods are chock-full of cleaning agents so powerful you can also use them to strip paint. Don't be fooled by the patented extra strength formula though, each packet of Yum-Yum Extra Strength Dishwasher Detergent looks and smells exactly like bubble gum. Because we here at Yum-Yum feel is it important to teach our little ones at an early age to help with household chores. That's why each box of Yum-Yum Extra Strength Dishwasher Detergent is specifically designed to look like your favorite box of breakfast cereal, so your children will surely enjoy loading and running the dishwasher. Each detergent pod is stamped with the famous laughing face of the Yum-Yum brand, so you know your washing your dishes with quality.

- Gynoculars: this is just one of those immature words that I came up with. That's all.

- Products that might not sell well #80
    - Doggy Darts
    - Garbage Can Collector sets 1-12
    - Doorless Microwave Oven
    - Seven count pumice sheets
    - Teletubbies Lighters, with easy-to-use push button igniter, collect all 50.
    - Powdered Beer
    - Swiss Army Shirt
    - Canned Bubblegum, pump or aerosol.
    - Hot Wheels Action Fireplace Set, with over thirty feet of track and the special non patented cast iron corkscrew U-turn that you place directly in the fireplace, jump the Ramp O' Death as your glowing red Hot Wheel exits the fiery pit! Jump over furniture, pillows, clothing, your little brother, or even your dad's box of fireworks.

- Ronald is a great name - for somebody else.

12

Spilled the Kool-Aid

- Isn't rebar a better name for bar-hopping? No? Okay.

- Let's play a game, It's called "Fireworks or Adult Film." Just try to guess which one it is by the title alone. Ready?

Super Load Space Charge
White Hot Streamers
The Screamer
Whole Rocket with Report
Double Bang Festival Balls
Lightning Rod
Bouncing Betty
Fire In the Hole
Dr. Bang
Dr. Boom
The Big Cracker Rocket
The Hummer
Big Ass Black Snake Rising
Red Palm
Golden Showers
Daddy Bucks
Uncle Sam's Blast Tube
Flash Bang
Poker Face
Invader Fountain

continued...........

Rising Missile
Big Bad Ass Bangers
Thunder Balls
Thar' She Blows
Bursting With Pride
Stinky Pete
Stick Party
Cracker Rock Banger
Nukes Of Hazard
Double Shot Hot Box
Kiss The Moon
The Whopper Rocket
The Shocker
Shooting Fun Stick
Barely Legal
Driller Thriller
She Bang
Black Hole
Desperate Attempt
Lady Fingers
Da Big Bad Bomb Box
Cherry Bomb / Pop Its
Ace In the Hole
Black Snakes XXL
All Night Long
Double Ball Breakers
Jumbo Mighty Cobra
Blown Away

continued...........

Nine Inch Fountain
Quad Banger
Magnum Popper
The Half Stick
Ball Exploder
Bombshell Intruder
One Hell of a Box
Screaming Gusher
Night Flasher

If you feel you got at least 90% correct, then you probably have already made the decision to become a pharmaceutical distributor.

- Here's a good idea, I think Taco Bell should run a promotional contest where the winner of the grand prize receives free menu items and gas for one year. But of course, the gas automatically comes with the eating. See where I went with that?

- What did Snoopy have against sleeping inside of his doghouse anyways? He chose to ruin his back by sleeping on the sharp peak of the roof.

- In this weeks episode of "HOW TO": We dive into the world of rap music, where we show you how to become a rap artist.

The first thing you need to do is write a rap song. It's easy, just come up with five words that rhyme - they do not have to relate to each other in any way, they only have to rhyme.

Now apply each word in a two-to-six-word sentence. don't worry about a story or a topic, The only underlining theme you will need to stick with is make sure every sentence has something to do with what you did, what you're going to do, what your like, or what you do not like.

Example:
1. Yoda
2. Toga
3. Yoga
4. Soda
5. Mota

"When I'm at a toga, I drink soda, not into Mota, or Yoga, and I lift shit like Yoda."

continued...........

See? Nice and easy. Now you need to look the part while rapping those lines. Grab something that resembles a microphone. I don't care what you use, it could be a carrot, a branch, a road flare, or even your Uncle Gil's prosthetic foot.

Now hold that "mic" close to your mouth with the butt end higher than your face and drape your index finger across your nose.

Now flail your other hand in a back-and-forth motion like you're polishing your dining room table with Lemon Fresh Pledge.

OK, you now have the song and the act, now you need the name. This is the easy part. Just take every fourth letter in your entire name and put them together to form an acronym. Now add one of the following six words and you've got your rap name.

-Monies
-Killa
-Dizzle
-Freak
-MuhFukka
-Billionaire

continued...........

Example:
If your name is Wilford Brimley your rap
name would be:
"F.B.L. Freak"
Alright, you now have what it takes to
become a rap artist.
That's all for "HOW TO"
Join us next week on "HOW TO,"
where we show you *How To* get rid of
hiccups with fireworks.

- Here's a few wonderful city slogans for
you.
> - "Welcome to Boise, Idaho. Fuck
> you."
> - "Tacoma, Washington. As seen on
> *Cops.*"
> - "Welcome to Billings, Montana. A
> great place to take a shit!"
> - "Del Rio, Texas. It kind of smells
> like hot urine here."

- Silence the deaf.........with mittens.

- Here is a merger of two great
musicians. Warren Buffett -"Werewolves
of Margaritaville."

- Up until the third grade I thought there were twenty-seven letters in the alphabet. I was sure that "&" was between the "Y" and the "Z"......QRS, TUV, WX, Y"&"Z, because that is how we all sang it. Alright, I wasn't a bright kid.

- What is it about being involved in a vehicle accident that makes you suddenly have to take a shit? Like right then and there. Gives a new meaning to the term "hit and run."

- Analysts in Britain have stated that the missing Malaysia Airlines flight MH370 left its final satellite ping approximately six thousand miles off course over the Southern Indian Ocean. Not to be outdone by this, officials in Hong Kong have claimed to have located and tracked over 14.3 million Ping's throughout Asia.

- Readers Poll: Which song is better? *Stairway to Heaven* or *Gimme Shelter*? Please email me your answer at StairwayToHeavenStinks@gmail.com

- I'm very excited! In just six days, I'm going to be having some reconstructive surgery done. I will have my shins lifted and then a little Botox added to my aura. I'm going to look eighteen again.

- It's common knowledge that dogs, cats, and many other animals, and now that I think about it, most men, mark their territory by urinating in the approximate area that they want to claim as their own. Which leads me to this question - did dinosaurs do that?

- Movie tidbit #9. Let's go all the way back to 1993, with a flick starring Johnny Depp. "What's Eating Gilbert Grape." Are you kidding me? Have you seen that movie? I think we all know who was doing all the eating.

-   If Jesus did CrossFit, then maybe his feet would have reached the ground and those nails wouldn't have been necessary. I guess it pays to get fitted for your cross. Hey, don't yell at me, I didn't come up with CrossFit.

-   There are two things wrong with printing instructions on containers of shampoo.
1. Every dang human that has the means to shower or bathe with some kind of form of soap that cleans your hair knows what to do with it.
2. The instructions say "lather, rinse, repeat." So, if you actually follow the instructions correctly, you will do that exact same shit over and over until the container is empty. Think about it.
Lather, rinse, repeat
Lather, rinse, repeat
Lather, rinse, repeat
Lather, rinse, repeat
Lather, rinse...........

Dog Poop for the Sole

ABOUT THE AUTHOR

Stan Nelson, the self-proclaimed master of pointless comedy in his neighborhood, likes wearing shorts and is told that he sounds like an orchestra when he sleeps.

When not writing, he is into scuba-walking, extreme yodeling, converting oxygen into carbon dioxide, and likes to bowl overhand.

He also travels around the U.S. to compete in High-Speed Quarter-Mile Hopscotch competitions.

Stan lives in the Puget Sound Region of Washington state with his wife, son, two dogs, and a cat that is into parkour.

But in all seriousness, he really does sound like an orchestra when he sleeps.

THANK YOU'S

*This is the part of the book that most people read first

First of all, an ultra-mega huge thanks to my wife Amanda and our son Parker, you both are awesome A.F. I can't even begin to thank you enough for everything you've done for me including encouraging my behavior. I love you.

Brian Michael Hall: I'm 94.793% sure that I would've never finished this book without your editing and layout skills, thank you for spending so much time listening to me whine about dots and spaces.

Bob Shook: a massive thank you for whipping up the cover, you graciously raised your hand when I asked for a volunteer. I know it wasn't easy. How bout' some bangers and mash and a game of Mastermind?

I am extremely grateful for these friends and family that gave me crucial feedback and inspiration along the way:

Fletcher Nelson, Dan Noble, Cory Carlson, John (Jason) Stefnik, David Salter, Stuart Nelson, Mike Gorman, Matt Love, Jeff Gilbert, Antonio J. Hopson, Ezekial Bonesteel.

And lastly, a big-ass bucket full of appreciation to YOU, the one holding this book right now. You are a gift to me.

Okay, it's time to go now. I had fun and I hope you did too.
Stay tuned, because there's more to come.......

Made in United States
Troutdale, OR
11/13/2024

24609893R00083